S0-GGN-928

# Lougawou

Copyright © 2017 Author Patrick Noze

Illustrated by, Patrick Noze

All rights reserved.

ISBN -10: 1547269103 ISBN-13: 9781547269105

# DEDICATION

This Book is dedicated to my Cousin Jocelyne Frederique and my 4 Brothers whom were present during these encounters. I am grateful for their presence in my life and the colorful memories we created during our youth.
Reginal Joseph, Jackie Joseph, Jude Robert Joseph and Vladimir Noze.

Special thanks to our Father Robert Noze , for providing us with a life style that permitted for the freedom to explore our surroundings.

# Lougawou

Growing up in Haiti in the summer of 1972 was one of the most beautiful moments  of my life. I lived with 4 of my brothers at my father's house all of us getting ready to go to various parts of the world. Amongst the oldest was Jocelyne our 19 year old cousin was in charge during fathers absence.

# PATRICK NOZE

# Lougawou

Every Sunday afternoon it was customary for us all to bade in the river  and then go home to get ready for a( PONPOM)  a short promenade around the town.  We all gathered in front of the house to determine which direction we will take. Jocelyne decided we would go the opposite direction from the house. A location we have never venture to before.

# PATRICK NOZE

All 6 of us began our journey that normally would end before dark. The afternoon was beautiful a typical Kenskoff afternoon with humming birds and a cool breeze that scattered the fragrance   of Jasmin in the atmosphere.

# Lougawou

We entered a part of the area we never knew existed , it is far into a wooded area. As we approach we notice a huge white house with giant Oak trees lined up on both sides of a long driveway. At the end of the driveway was the House. Suddenly we heard a  big Dog barking a very loud. The dog came from the second floor balcony of the house and started chasing us. We ran faster than light.

# Patrick Noze

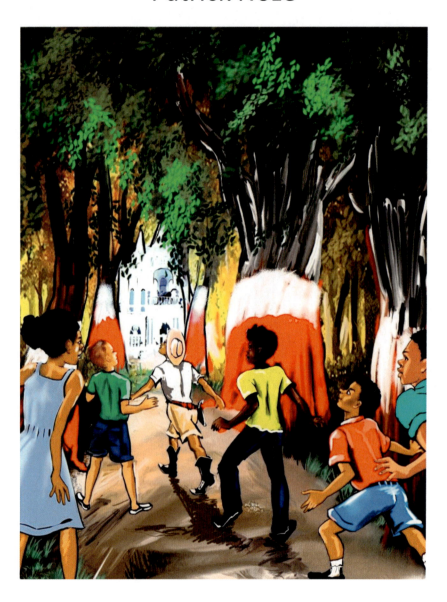

## Lougawou

We ran so far that we got to the other side of a mountain leading to a road that leads to father's restaurant.

# Lougawo

By now it was starting to get dark. On the road we noticed a man standing under an electric pole . The closer we got to the man the taller he became.  He was a "MET MINWI" (The Midnight Master) Suddenly the church bell strikes midnight. When we looked back the man disappear from thin air.

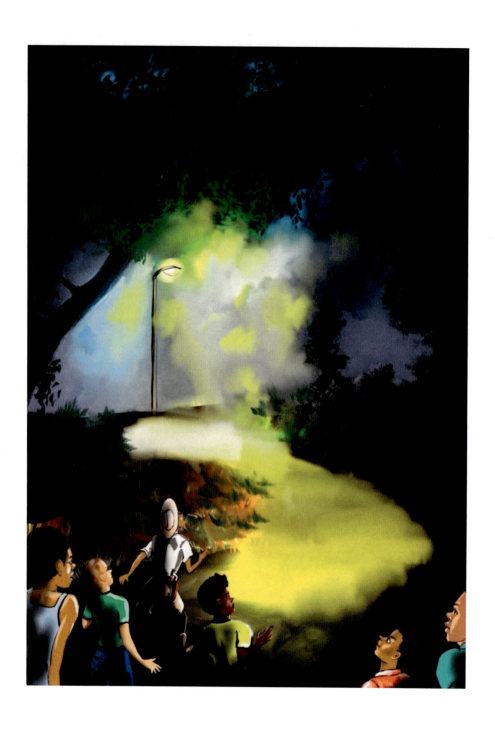

We were now at father's Restaurant feeling a since of relief thinking we were safe when a flash of light went flying  from above our heads. In panic we started knocking on the metal gates of the restaurants. Hoping the guardian of the property would open the gate.

Again the flash of light

went flying this time closer from above our head. Jocelyne dropped to her knees and begin to pray meanwhile the object flying in a cross formation created a cross of fire as if to mock us.

14

It then hover in the center of the cross staring down at us. It was a man with half of his body engulfed in flame with his arms spread out like wings.

As we pray on our knees all crunched up holding each other and looking up. We heard the horn of a car. It was father. The head lights of His car blinding our view.

When we looked up again the Lougawou ( Boogie man)  was gone We never spoke of that night till now.

About the Author :

Patrick Noze
Born in Haiti in December 11,1962 in the province of Jeremie 'City of Poets'.
Patrick Noze was introduced to the world of art years before achieving International success, by way of his father, Robert Noze. Robert had his own art history as a renown Sculptor. He studied under his father, Andre Dimanche, making Patrick Noze a third generation Sculptor and painter.

At the age of 5, Patrick's father, presented him with a box containing oil paint and brushes; and he has never stop painting . Patrick became recognized as an artist at the age of 12 . After painting his rendition of a painting entitled ('Rara') , a celebration of pass over within the Haitian culture. His father overwhelmed with his first attempt, sold the painting for $50.00 to a tourist who fell in love with his laymen application of colors. Patrick Noze specializes in subjects ranging from realism, surrealism , impressionism, abstract, sculpture and portraits.
"I am always thinking about the wonders of the world from its simplest to its most complex shapes. To my eyes, the world is a large canvas. Everything I see, dream or I encounter I use as an inspiration for my work.

In 1976 I entered the United States and begins studying art, through private lessons at the School of Visual Arts in New York where I concentrated in anatomy and color techniques. In 1979 I entered Franklin Delano Roosevelt, High school majoring in Fine Arts with a focus in Painting and sculpture. Upon graduation I received, the "Delano Metal of Honor, with a full scholarship to Cooper Union. However, I declined and attended Pratt Institute, School of Art and Science. While there I Majored in fine arts with a minor in education. Presently I am very involved in my community and serve on a voluntary basis on the Advisory Council for Art in Cultural Affairs. In Orange County, Florida.

# FIN

Made in United States
Orlando, FL
07 February 2024

43405730R00018